Book of Mormon Stories for Little Children

Book of Mormon Stories for Little Children

Marjorie G. Johnson

Eighth Printing: March 2005

International Standard Book Number
0-88290-063-3

Horizon Publishers' Catalog and Order Number
C1310

Printed and distributed
in the United States of America by

& Distributors, Incorporated

Address:

925 North Main Street

Springville, Utah 84663

Local Phone: (801) 489-4084
WATS (toll free): 1 (800) SKYBOOK
FAX: (800) 489-1097

Contents

Marjorie G. Johnson

"We are going to Primary, would you like to come along?"

As a little girl, Marjorie Guinn responded to the invitation of her friends and went to Primary. The spirit of love and tenderness so overwhelmed her that she asked if she might also attend Sunday School. As she walked through the doors of the rented hall where Sunday School was being held, the Spirit whispered, "This is the true Church." And so, at the age of ten, Marjorie was baptized.

In the little branch of the Church in Ajo, Arizona, she began teaching Sunday School and Primary in her early teens. For thirty years she has taught the gospel to children and youth, not only in the classroom, but also as chorister and organist for various church organizations.

She has written many stories and songs for her own children as well as for Church programs. She and her husband, Fred G. Johnson, Jr., are the parents of six sons.

She has attended Brigham Young University, Mesa Community College and Arizona State University, majoring in education and music.

Because her introduction to the gospel was through the Primary, Sister Johnson is aware of the great missionary potential of little children. "What a blessing it is to be a teacher of these little missionaries!"

7

My Book of Mormon Song

Marjorie Johnson

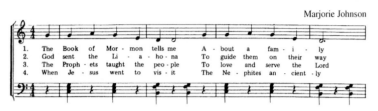

1. The Book of Mor - mon tells me   A - bout a fam - i - ly
2. God sent the Li - a - ho - na   To guide them on their way
3. The Proph - ets taught the peo - ple   To love and serve the Lord
4. When Je - sus went to vis - it   The Ne - phites an - cient - ly

Who left dear old Je - ru - sa - lem and sailed a - cross the sea
It worked when they were right - eous and when they did o - bey
To treat their neigh - bors kind - ly and al - ways keep His word
He blessed the lit - tle chil - dren and held them on His knee

Le - hi was their fa - ther Their proph - et and their chief
Ne - phi made the Gold - en plates He wrote the Lord's com - mand
La - man - ites and Ne - phites Had wars in their new land
When He comes to earth a - gain I hope that I will be

He fol - lowed God's com - mand - ments Be - cause of his be - lief.
He tried to keep things peace - ful Going to the prom - ised land.
When they for - got to lis - ten And keep the Lord's com - mand.
The kind of child that He will love And bless e - ter - nal - ly.

Chorus

The Book of Mor - mon tells me Of proph - ets brave and true

It tells a - bout the Sav - ior, And His Love for me and you.

The Prophet Lehi

Many years ago, long before Jesus was born, a prophet lived in Jerusalem. The prophet's name was Lehi. His wife's name was Sariah. They had four sons: Laman, Lemuel, Sam, and Nephi.

Many people in Jerusalem were very wicked. Lehi told the people, "You are not keeping Heavenly Father's laws. You should repent of your sins and choose the right."

Some of the people were very angry with Lehi for talking to them that way. They wanted to hurt Lehi.

One day, Heavenly Father said, "Lehi, it's not safe for you to live in Jerusalem anymore. The people are angry because you told them to repent. Take your family and move to the desert."

Lehi preached to the people of Jerusalem.

Father Lehi was a rich man. He had a beautiful home, pretty jewels, and a lot of money. Lehi knew they would be in the desert for many years. He knew they could not take their jewels or their money with them.

Laman and Lemuel were very unhappy. They did not want to leave their nice things. They loved their beautiful home and sparkling jewels more than they loved the Lord.

Nephi and Sam were glad to obey their father.

Lehi hoped Laman and Lemuel would try to be happy in their desert home.

———

He did as the Lord commanded him.
I Nephi 2:3

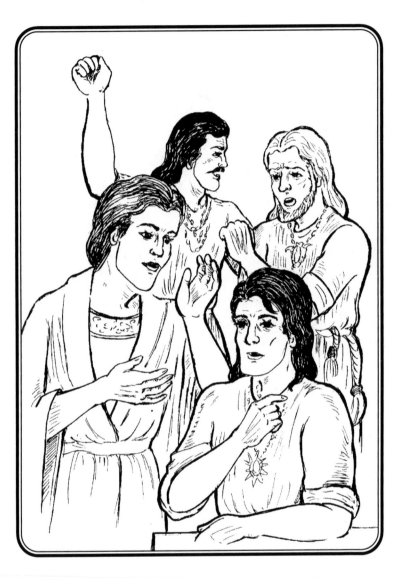

Laman and Lemuel were wicked,
but Sam and Nephi were good.

The Book

Lehi moved his family out into the desert, as the Lord commanded.

One day, Heavenly Father spoke to Lehi again. He told Lehi to send his sons back to Jerusalem to get their family book from a man named Laban. This book was written on square plates made of metal. It was very important to take this book with them. It told about Heavenly Father's laws and the prophets. It had many of the same stories in it that the Bible has. They called this book the brass plates.

"We don't want to go," said Laman and Lemuel. "It is very foolish to go all the way back just to get a book. Besides, someone might try to hurt us."

"The Lord will protect you," said Father Lehi. "You must go and help get the book."

Nephi showed the brass plates to his family.

Nephi said, "I will do anything Heavenly Father wants me to do. He will help us keep His commandments."

And He did. Heavenly Father helped Nephi and his brothers get the book and take it back to their father, Lehi.

Lehi was very happy to get the book. He sat right down and read it. He found it told wonderful true stories about their family and their ancestors. He knew this book would help them to keep Heavenly Father's commandments.

I will go and do the things which the Lord hath commanded. 1 Nephi 3:7

17

Ishmael's family decided to
travel with Lehi's family.

Ishmael and His Family

Heavenly Father knew that Lehi and his family would be in the desert for many years. Lehi's sons, Laman, Lemuel, Sam, and Nephi, were grown-up young men now. These young men should have wives so they could start their own families.

Heavenly Father told Lehi to send his sons back to Jerusalem again. He wanted them to go see a man named Ishmael. Ishmael was one of Lehi's very good friends.

Some of Ishmael's children were lovely grown-up girls. These girls would make good wives for Lehi's sons.

Nephi and his brothers went back to Jerusalem to see Ishmael. They told him about Heavenly Father's commandments to their father, Lehi.

*The children of Lehi and
Ishmael married each other.*

Nephi said, "If we are faithful, Heavenly Father will lead us to a promised land. Do you want to go with us?"

Ishmael and his family talked it over. "Yes," said Ishmael, "we will go with you."

They wanted to go, but they were sad because they knew they would never see Jerusalem again.

They traveled in the desert and came to the place where Father Lehi was living in his tent.

Soon Nephi and his brothers married the beautiful daughters of Ishmael.

———

If we are faithful to Him, we shall obtain the land of promise. 1 Nephi 7:13

Lehi dreamed of the
tree of life and the iron rod.

Lehi's Dream

Heavenly Father talks to His prophets in many different ways. Sometimes He talks out loud to them. Sometimes He whispers to them with a still small voice. Sometimes He gives them very special dreams, called visions.

While Lehi was living in the desert, Heavenly Father gave him a very special dream. In this dream he saw a tree in a big field. He saw a narrow path leading to the tree. He saw an iron rod beside the path.

He also saw the people of the world. They were stumbling along in a dark fog. Many people were getting lost. Others were trying to find the narrow path that leads to the tree. They wanted to get to the tree because it was the tree of life.

We hold onto the iron rod by
keeping God's commandments.

He saw some of the people hold onto the iron rod. By holding onto the iron rod, they could stay on the path and get to the tree of life.

In Lehi's dream, the tree of life is Eternal Life.

The narrow path is the road that leads to Eternal Life.

The iron rod is the word of God.

When we obey God's laws, we are holding onto the iron rod.

When we obey God's laws, we are on the path leading to Heavenly Father and Eternal Life.

―――――――

The iron rod is the word of God.
1 Nephi 15:23-24

The Liahona showed Nephi
where they should go.

The Liahona

We are Heavenly Father's children and He loves us very much. When we have problems, we can pray to Heavenly Father and He will guide us.

The Bible tells us about the children of Israel going to a promised land. Heavenly Father guided them with a cloud of smoke by day and a cloud of fire by night.

Lehi was taking his people to a different promised land. Heavenly Father gave something very special to Lehi to guide him. It was a compass.

This compass was made of brass and was round like a ball. It had needles in it like a compass. One needle pointed the way they should go.

When the people were good, the compass showed them which way they should go. When the people were bad, it did not work at all.

This compass has a name. It is called Liahona.

And it did work for them according to their faith in God. Alma 37:40

Nephi Breaks His Bow

As they traveled in the desert, Lehi and Ishmael had families of children and grandchildren. These families had many problems to solve as they went along. One very big problem was finding enough food for everyone. Very little food grew in the desert so Heavenly Father told them to kill wild animals for food.

One time when Nephi and his brothers were hunting for food, Nephi broke his bow. His brothers were having trouble making their bows work right. Everything was going wrong. Laman and Lemuel thought it was all Nephi's fault. They were very angry with Nephi.

Nephi said, "Laman and Lemuel, you must stop complaining. Have faith and Heavenly Father will help us."

Nephi needed his bow to bring home food.

Nephi talked to his brothers for a long time. Then Laman and Lemuel felt sorry they had been angry. They prayed and asked Heavenly Father to help them.

Nephi made a new bow out of wood. He made some arrows out of sticks. Then he looked in the compass, or Liahona, to see which way he should go to find food.

This time when he went hunting, everything went right. He found many wild animals.

The people were very happy to have so much food to eat. They gave thanks to Heavenly Father.

―――――――

They did humble themselves
before the Lord. 1 Nephi 16:32

Jacob and Joseph

The families of Lehi and Ishmael grew as they traveled together. The journey lasted for eight years. Many boys and girls grew up traveling in the desert. Many babies were born as they traveled.

Two of these babies were little baby boys born to Lehi and Sariah. They named these boys Jacob and Joseph.

Jacob and Joseph learned to love the Lord while they were very young. They also loved their brother Nephi. They watched him go hunting and bring food into their camp.

They listened when he talked to the people about Heavenly Father's goodness.

They helped him with his work.

They wanted to grow up to be strong and good like Nephi.

Jacob and Joseph loved Nephi and the Lord.

Lehi said to Jacob and Joseph, "Always be good like your brother, Nephi, and you will always be happy."

If there be no righteousness, there can be no happiness. 2 Nephi 2:13

Nephi Builds A Ship

After eight long years of traveling in the desert, Lehi and his people finally came to a beautiful seashore. They named the land Bountiful because there was so much good fruit to eat. They called the sea Irreantum, which means "many waters."

Heavenly Father told Nephi to build a ship so they could cross the many waters and go to the promised land.

Laman and Lemuel laughed at Nephi.

"Nephi, you are foolish," said Laman and Lemuel. "You can't build a ship. You have never built a ship. You don't know how." So they laughed and laughed.

"You are right," said Nephi. "I have never built a ship before. But Heavenly Father told me to build one. I know He will help me. He will show me how to make the tools and how to cut the wood. He will show me how to make it tight so no water will come in.

Nephi and his brothers built a ship.

Heavenly Father told Laman and Lemuel to be good and to help Nephi build the ship.

Then they all worked together and built a big ship. When it was ready, all the people went into the ship. They sailed on the water for a long time. At last they landed on the shore of the promised land.

Do you know the name of the promised land? It is America. That is where Nephi's ship landed.

———

He that is righteous is favored of God.
1 Nephi 17:35

They sailed to America, the promised land.

The Nephites and Lamanites

Nephi was happy to be in this beautiful land of promise. He knew this would always be a land of liberty to those who live righteously. He hoped that his brothers would choose the right and serve the Lord.

Laman and Lemuel did not choose the right. They would not listen to the words of the Lord. Sometimes they were very mean to Nephi and the other good people.

One night, Heavenly Father told Nephi to gather all the good people together. He told them to move away from Laman and Lemuel. All the people who wanted to serve the Lord followed Nephi. From then on they were called Nephites.

The people who did not want to serve the Lord stayed with Laman and Lemuel. They were called Lamanites.

Heavenly Father gave the Lamanites a darker skin. The Indians who live in the Americas today are descendants of the Lamanites.

The Lamanites became wicked and wild.

The Nephites worked and built a temple.

The Nephites built houses and planted gardens in their new home. They also built a temple where they could serve the Lord.

Heavenly Father blessed them and they were very happy. They were glad to have a new home in this land of promise.

———

O how great the plan of our God!
2 Nephi 9:13

King Benjamin

Many years after the Nephites moved away from the Lamanites, they lived in a city called Zarahemla. They had a very good king. His name was King Benjamin. He loved and served his people well. He did not tax the people. They did not have to give him money, or food, or cattle, or anything. He did his work with his own hands.

King Benjamin was a prophet who loved the Lord. When he was very old, he said to his helpers, "Please ask the people to gather around the temple for a meeting."

When the people came, King Benjamin climbed on a high tower and spoke to them. He told them that Heavenly Father loved them very much.

He asked the people, "Do you love Heavenly Father?"

*King Benjamin taught his people
to love one another.*

"Yes," said the people, "we do love Heavenly Father."

"Do you want to show Heavenly Father that you love Him?" asked King Benjamin.

"Yes," said the people.

"Then you must love one another," said King Benjamin, "and you must serve one another."

When the meeting was over, the people promised to love one another.

Soon after the meeting, King Benjamin died. His son Mosiah became the new king of the Nephites at Zarahemla.

———

Love one another and serve one another.
Mosiah 4:15

Wicked King Noah

Most of the time the Nephites were good people, but sometimes some of them forgot to be good. King Noah was a Nephite who was very bad. He was so bad that people called him Wicked King Noah.

In his land there was a prophet named Abinadi. The Prophet Abinadi was a very brave man. He told King Noah to repent of his sins.

"King Noah," the prophet said, "you drink too much wine. You take too much money from the people. You do not love the Lord. You must repent or Heavenly Father will punish you for being so wicked."

King Noah did not repent. He did not want to be good. He was very angry with Abinadi for telling him the truth. He told his helpers to kill the prophet Abinadi.

Abinadi warned King Noah
he was doing wrong.

Heavenly Father was very unhappy with King Noah. He punished King Noah just as Abinadi said He would. The Lamanites came into the land. King Noah's people ran away. They got angry with King Noah and finally killed him.

King Noah ran away when
the Lamanites attacked.

He shall know that I am the Lord.
Mosiah 12:3

Alma and His People

One of King Noah's helpers was named Alma. Alma listened to the Prophet Abinadi and believed his words. Alma was sorry for the sins he had committed and he repented.

Alma began to preach the gospel to the people. Soon he gathered all the good people together and left King Noah's country.

At first they went to a beautiful lake in the forest called the Waters of Mormon. Here Alma baptized the good people who followed him.

Soon they moved to another place where they could build a city. They named their new city Helam.

After a little while, some Lamanites moved in and took over the city of Helam. Alma and his people were forced to be slaves for the Lamanites.

Alma baptized the people
at the Waters of Mormon.

48

The people prayed and asked Heavenly Father to help them. Heavenly Father answered their prayers. One night He made the Lamanite guards fall asleep. Alma and his people quietly walked past the sleeping guards and left the city of Helam.

Alma and his people traveled to Zarahemla.

They traveled for twelve days and finally came to the "land of Zarahemla; and King Mosiah did receive them with joy."

*None could deliver them but
the Lord their God. Mosiah 23:23*

Alma the Younger and the Sons of Mosiah

Alma and his people had escaped from the Lamanites. They were happy to be living in the land of Zarahemla with King Mosiah. Here they were free to care for their families and to serve the Lord.

As Alma's children grew up, not all of them loved the Lord. One of Alma's sons was called Alma the Younger. Alma the Younger and four of the sons of King Mosiah were bad boys. They caused a lot of trouble in the churches. Alma and King Mosiah were very sad.

They asked Heavenly Father to help their boys to be good. One day when the boys were out causing trouble, a very surprising thing happened. An angel of the Lord appeared to them!

*An angel appeared to Alma's son
and the sons of King Mosiah.*

The angel told them to repent. The angel spoke with so much power that the boys fell down to the ground.

After the angel left, Alma the Younger could not speak or move. His friends carried him to his father.

When Alma could speak again, he said, "An angel came from God and told me to be good. I have repented of my sins. Now I want to be a missionary."

From that time on, Alma the Younger and the four sons of King Mosiah were very good missionaries. They loved the Lord and served Him all their lives.

———

How blessed are they! For they did publish peace. Mosiah 27:37

Alma the Younger, A Missionary

Alma the Younger went on a mission to the Nephites who lived in Ammonihah. The people in Ammonihah were wicked. They had forgotten to love the Lord. They had forgotten to keep His laws.

Alma met Amulek there and they preached the gospel to the people.

"Repent," said Alma. "Repent now or you will be destroyed."

The people in Ammonihah did not believe anything Alma and Amulek told them. They threw the missionaries into jail and tied them with ropes. Alma and Amulek were in jail for several days. The judges were mean to them. They slapped them. They did not give them enough food.

*Alma and Amulek were kept
safe by Heavenly Father.*

At last Heavenly Father gave the missionaries extra strength. They broke the ropes that tied them. The building began to shake. The walls fell down and killed the wicked people in the building.

But Alma and Amulek walked out of the ruined prison unhurt. When the wicked people saw them they were frightened. They ran away and let the missionaries go free.

———

Alma and Amulek came forth out of the prison and they were not hurt.
Alma 14:28

Ammon and King Lamoni

Ammon was one of the sons of King Mosiah. He had seen an angel and wanted to be a good missionary. He asked his father if he could go teach the gospel to the Lamanites.

King Mosiah said, "Go, my son. The Lord will protect you."

Ammon went to the land of Ishmael. He became a servant of the Lamanite king, Lamoni. His first job was to help protect the King's sheep. While he and some other servants were tending the sheep, some robbers came. The other servants were afraid and ran away, but Ammon stayed and fought. Heavenly Father gave him extra strength and he frightened the robbers away.

King Lamoni was pleased to learn that his new servant was so brave and strong. Ammon

*Ammon fought the robbers and
took care of the king's sheep.*

became good friends with King Lamoni and he taught the gospel to the King.

The King was happy to learn that he had a Heavenly Father who loved him. The King gave Ammon the right to preach to gospel to everyone in his land.

———————

The King believed all his words.
Alma 19:40

Ammon told King Lamoni
about Heavenly Father.

The Lamanites Bury Their Swords

After the missionary, Ammon, visited the Lamanite king, Lamoni, many Lamanites joined the Church. They felt very sorry for the wrong things they had done. They promised they would never fight again.

They took their swords and buried them deep in the ground. After they did this they were called the people of God.

Some of their Lamanite cousins were angry to see these Lamanites choosing the right. The bad Lamanites began to fight the good people.

The people of God would not fight back. They had promised the Lord they would not fight so they didn't. They lay down on the ground when the bad Lamanites came to hurt them.

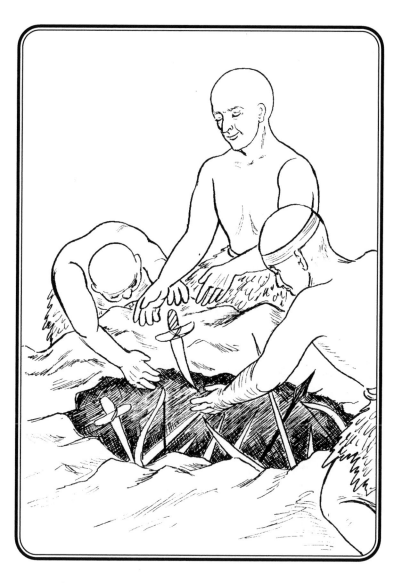

The good Lamanites buried their swords
so they wouldn't kill others.

The bad Lamanites were very surprised. "See the people of God," they said. "They would rather die than break their promise to God."

The bad Lamanites stopped fighting. "Tell us more about this God you love so much," they said.

Then the people of God told their cousins all about Heavenly Father and how much he loves us. After that many of the bad Lamanites repented and joined the church.

Heavenly Father told Ammon to take King Lamoni and his people to Zarahemla. The Nephites welcomed them and called them "the people of Ammon."

———————

They took their swords . . . and did bury them. Alma 24:17-30

The 2,000 Sons of Helaman

For many years the people of Ammon lived with the Nephites. The Nephites protected them and they were brothers in the Church.

Soon the bad Lamanites began causing trouble in the land. The Nephites needed more soldiers. The people of Ammon could not be soldiers because they had promised the Lord they would never fight again.

The Ammonites had 2,000 young sons who wanted to be soldiers. They said, "Our fathers promised never to fight again, but we did not. Let us be soldiers. We will fight for the liberty of our fathers."

The mothers of these young boys loved them tenderly. They were sad to see them going off to war. Through the Spirit of the Lord, these

The Lamanite mothers taught
their sons to trust God.

mothers made this promise to their sons: "If you have faith in the Lord and keep all of His commandments, you will come home safely."

These young men asked a righteous man named Helaman to be their leader. Helaman loved these boys and called them his sons. The sons of Helaman fought bravely and protected the liberty of their fathers. All during the war they kept the Lord's commandments.

How happy and thankful the mothers were at the end of the war! All 2,000 of the young men returned home safely, just as Heavenly Father had promised.

They do put their trust in God.
Alma 57:27

The Title of Liberty

Moroni was a Nephite Captain. He was also a man who loved our Heavenly Father. His people were good and at this time they were free. Captain Moroni wanted them to stay free.

He was very worried about them because the Lamanites were in the borders of the land. The Lamanites wanted to take over the country.

Captain Moroni thought of a way to gather all the Nephites together. He said, "My people need a flag!" So he tore a big piece of cloth from his coat and made a flag from it.

Does your country have a flag? What are the colors in your flag? We do not know what color Captain Moroni's flag was, but we do know he wrote some words on it. This is what it said:

> In memory of our God . . . our religion and freedom. . . and our peace . . . our wives . . . our children.

*Captain Moroni made a flag
called the "Title of Liberty."*

The Nephites fought to keep their country free.

Captain Moroni called his flag *The Title of Liberty.* He put the flag on a pole and carried it through the land so all the people could see it.

He said, "All of you who want to stay free from the Lamanites, follow me." So many people followed Captain Moroni that the Lamanites were frightened away.

Let us preserve our liberty.
Alma 46:24

68

Samuel the Lamanite

Most of the prophets in the Book of Mormon were Nephites, but one was a Lamanite. He was a very important prophet named Samuel. When Samuel was a prophet, some of the Lamanites were good but most of the Nephites were bad.

One day Heavenly Father said, "Samuel, go preach to the Nephites."

So Samuel went to Zarahemla where the Nephites lived. He stood on their city wall and talked to them. Samuel said, "In just five more years, Jesus will be born among the Jews. The night before He is born there will be no darkness. A beautiful new star will appear in the sky. There will be a day, and a night that is light as day and another day. It will seem like one long day. This will be the sign of His birth."

The wicked people
didn't believe Samuel's words.

70

*Heavenly Father kept Samuel safe
from the rocks and arrows.*

71

The Nephites were angry with Samuel for telling them to repent. They tried to hurt him. Heavenly Father protected Samuel. When the Nephites threw rocks and spears, and shot arrows at Samuel, they always missed him.

Samuel gave his message to the Nephites. Then he jumped down off the city wall and went back to his own country.

Some of the Nephites believed what Samuel said. They went to their own prophet and asked to be baptized. They began to say, "We must live righteously so we will be ready when Jesus comes to visit us.

———————

Prepare the way of the Lord.
Helaman 14:9

A New Star

The Nephites remembered the words of Samuel, the Lamanite prophet: "Jesus will be born in five more years." The Nephites counted the days and the years, waiting and waiting for the sign of the birth of Jesus.

The Nephites waited for Christ to be born.

A new star appeared when Jesus was born.

74

Finally, after five years of waiting, the sign was given. The night before Jesus was born, a very bright new star appeared in the sky. When the sun went down, it was so light it seemed like there was no night at all. The sky was very bright with a beautiful light. Then all the people knew that Jesus was born.

The good people were very happy to see the sign of His birth. Many of their friends asked to be baptized and they became members of the Church. The people were happy to see the new star in the sky.

They were happy to know that Jesus was born. They said, "Maybe some day we will see Jesus."

A new star did appear. 3 Nephi 1:21

The Birth of Jesus

When Heavenly Father plans to do anything special on the earth, He always tells His prophets what He is going to do. He told many prophets that someday He would send His Son to earth.

Six hundred years before Jesus was born in Bethlehem, the prophet Nephi had a special dream, called a vision.

In this vision he saw Mary, the mother of Jesus. He saw that she was very fair and white, and that she was a beautiful young girl.

She was kind and gentle. Heavenly Father knew she would be a very good mother. She loved her Heavenly Father and said she would do anything He asked her to do.

She was happy to be the mother of Jesus.

Nephi had seen Jesus and
his mother, Mary, in a vision.

77

Nephi was shown this beautiful vision so he could tell his people about the birth of the Savior. Through the ages, the people looked forward to the time when Jesus would really be born. It made the people happy to hear this story.

Nephi wrote the story down in the Book of Mormon and we can read it today.

———

He shall be called Jesus Christ, the Son of God. Mosiah 3:8

Jesus Is Risen

The prophets had told the people many things about Jesus. They told the people about the new star when Jesus was born. The prophets told the people that Jesus would be crucified and then resurrected. They said, "When Jesus dies, there will be three days of darkness."

The good people were watching for the sign. One day it happened. The sun did not shine. The bad people were afraid, but the good people knew that Heavenly Father would protect them.

Awful things happened during the darkness. The earth shook, buildings fell down, and people were crying.

Then something wonderful happened. They heard a voice from Heaven. They listened and watched very carefully.

*Jesus came down from
heaven to visit the people.*

*The people were excited
and very happy to see Jesus.*

The voice came again saying, "Behold my Beloved Son, in whom I am well pleased."

Soon they saw a light. The light became bigger and brighter. Someone was in the light. As He came closer and closer they could see that it was Jesus.

"Jesus is risen from the dead," said the people, "and He is coming to see us."

They were happy to see Jesus.

———

I am the light and life
of the world. 3 Nephi 9:18

Jesus and the Nephites

The Nephites were very happy to be with Jesus. He talked to them and told them how to live righteously.

He asked them, "Have you any that are sick among you?"

*Jesus blessed the sick people
and made them well.*

"Yes," said the people, "some of our people are sick."

"Bring them to me," said Jesus. Then He blessed the sick people and made them well.

Then He called their little children to Him. He put His arms around them and blessed them. After He blessed the children, Jesus said, "Behold your little ones."

Jesus talked to the little children and blessed them.

The people looked and saw the angels from heaven come down. They made a bright circle around the children and gave them more blessings.

*Angels from heaven came
down by the children.*

Jesus taught the people about the sacrament. He said, "When you take the sacrament, remember me. Remember that I love you and want you to keep Heavenly Father's commandments."

Jesus told the people to always love one another.

The people loved Jesus with all their hearts and were very happy that Jesus had come to visit them.

Jesus taught the people about the sacrament.

Behold your little ones. 3 Nephi 17:23

Jared and His People

The Book of Mormon tells about another group of people who came to America. These people were called the Jaredites. They came to America more than a thousand years before the prophets Lehi and Nephi.

In the Bible we read the story about the Tower of Babel. At that time most of the people were wicked, but a few were good. Jared was the leader of the good people. He wanted to take his people to a better place.

Jared said to his brother, who was the prophet, "Ask Heavenly Father to take us away from these wicked people."

Heavenly Father led them to a place by the ocean. He said to the brother of Jared, "Make eight boats that will be so tight no water or light

The brother of Jared wanted to move his family away from wicked people.

can get in after the door is shut. You will cross a big ocean and it will take a long time, so take your food with you."

Jared was happy for all the help that Heavenly Father had given them but he was worried about something. He said to his brother, "It will be very dark in our boats. We will not be able to see each other. When we move around in the dark we might step on our little children. Please ask Heavenly Father to give us some light."

The brother of Jared went to the mountain and found 16 special stones. He asked Heavenly Father to make them shine. The Lord touched the stones with His finger and the stones made a bright shining light. The brother of Jared placed two shining stones in each boat. The people were very happy to have lights in their boats. Then they safely crossed the ocean to America, their new home.

―――――

In me shall all mankind have light.
Ether 3:14

The Lord made the stones shine
so there would be light in the boats.

The Book of Mormon

Through the years, the prophets wrote a book about the Nephites and the Lamanites. Nephi was the first prophet to write in the book. Each prophet in his turn wrote something.

This book was different from our books. It was not made of paper. It was made of thin, square pages of gold. The prophets did not write with ink. They used a sharp tool, like a big nail, and scratched words on the gold pages. This book of gold is called the golden plates.

Many years after Jesus came to America, a prophet named Mormon took care of the golden plates. Before the prophet Mormon died, he gave the plates to his son Moroni.

Moroni was the last prophet to write on the golden plates. Heavenly Father told Moroni that some day you and I could read all of these stories.

Moroni buried the gold plates
in the hill Cumorah.

The stories from the golden plates are in a book called *The Book of Mormon.*

We are glad Heavenly Father gave us The Book of Mormon. It tells us about the Nephites and the Lamanites. It tells us about Jesus coming to America. It helps us to understand the Bible.

Moroni tells us that if we read and pray about it, Heavenly Father will let us know that *The Book of Mormon* is true.

———

Ask God, the Eternal Father,
in the name of Christ,
if these things are true. Moroni 10:4

Heavenly Father will show us
the Book of Mormon is true.

94